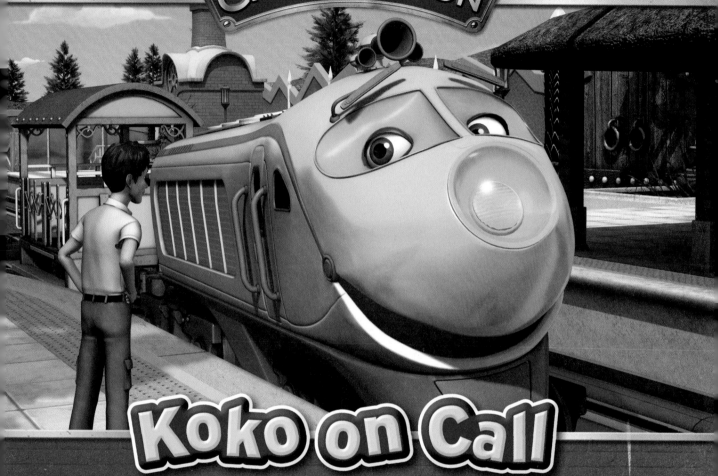

Koko on Call

Adapted by Michael Anthony Steele
Based on the story by Brenda Scott Royce

SCHOLASTIC INC.
New York   Toronto   London   Auckland
Sydney   Mexico City   New Delhi   Hong Kong

ISBN 978-0-545-26633-8

12 11 10 9 8 7 6 5 4 3 2   11 12 13 14 15 16/0

Printed in the U.S.A.   40
First printing, April 2011

Koko rolled into the train depot. "I finished all my work, Vee!" she said.

"Good job, Koko," said Vee, the depot's announcer. "I have one more job for you. I need a speedy chugger to help Dr. Gosling at the Safari Park."

"I'm the speediest!" said Koko.

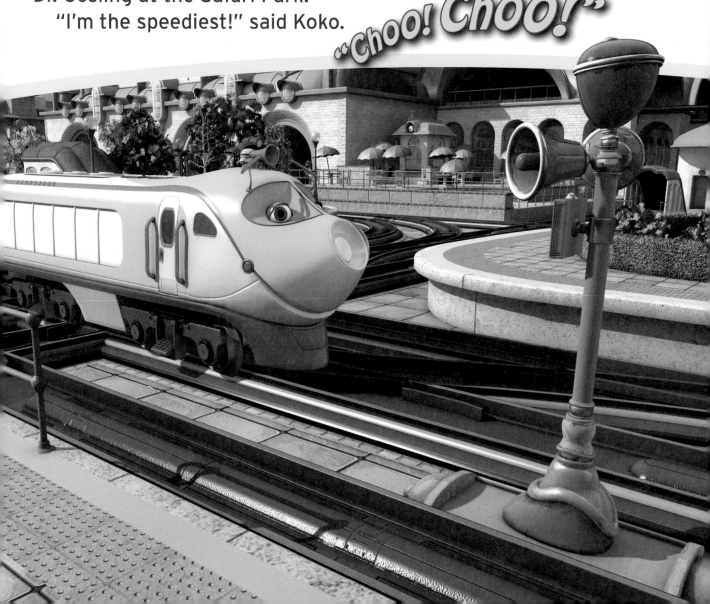

"Choo! Choo!"

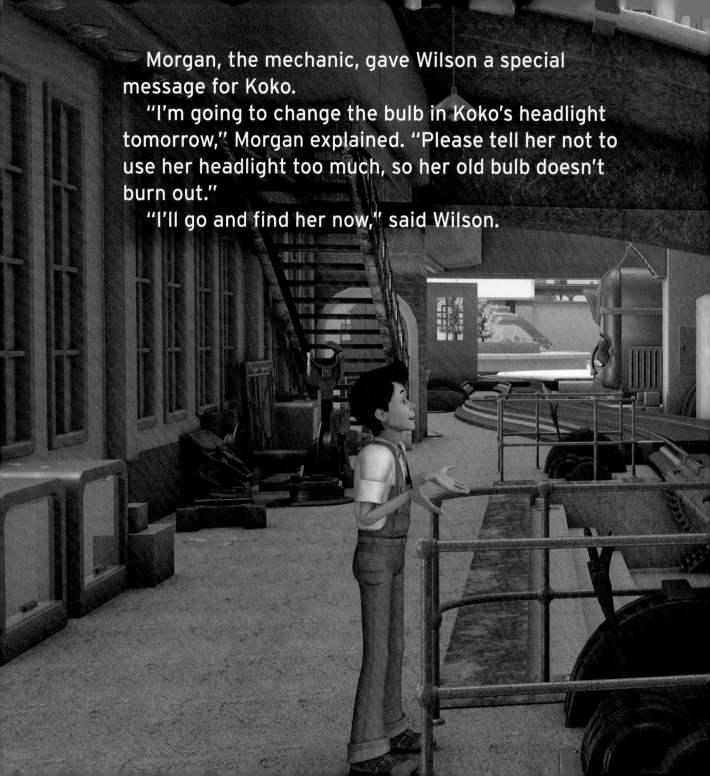

Morgan, the mechanic, gave Wilson a special message for Koko.

"I'm going to change the bulb in Koko's headlight tomorrow," Morgan explained. "Please tell her not to use her headlight too much, so her old bulb doesn't burn out."

"I'll go and find her now," said Wilson.

When Koko arrived at the Safari Park, Dr. Gosling had big news.

"Twiga, the giraffe, is getting ready to have a baby," the doctor explained. "If she starts to have the baby tonight, I need you to come to my house to get me."

"You can count on me!" said Koko.
"Let's go to my house now," said Dr. Gosling.
"I'll show you how to get there."

As Koko carried Dr. Gosling home, they passed some flowers. "They smell so good!" she said.

"Turn here, Koko," Dr. Gosling instructed.

"Now cross the bridge over the stream," the doctor said.

Koko could hear the stream's water rushing underneath her. As she crossed the bridge, she felt her wheels go *clickety-clack, clickety-clack.*

"We're here!" Dr. Gosling said as they pulled in front of his house. "Can you please pick me up here later, Koko?"

"Will do," she replied.

Koko returned to the Safari Park to find Wilson waiting for her. He had to tell her about her headlight.
"Twiga is going to have a baby!" Koko exclaimed.
She started telling Wilson all about her job for the night.

"**Wowser!**" said Wilson.
He was so excited to hear about the baby giraffe
that he forgot all about Morgan's message for Koko.

That night, Mtambo joined Koko at the park. An owl hooted overhead. "That owl is awake because he is a nocturnal animal," said Mtambo.

"Whoo! Whoo!"

"Nocturnal?" asked Koko.

"Nocturnal animals sleep in the day and are awake at night," Mtambo explained. "Since it's hard to see at night, they use their noses to smell and their ears to hear. Some even feel their way through the night."

Long after Mtambo left, Koko heard Twiga get to her feet and make a strange sound.

"I think it's time," said Koko. "Don't worry, Twiga. I'll be back with Dr. Gosling in two clickety-clacks!"

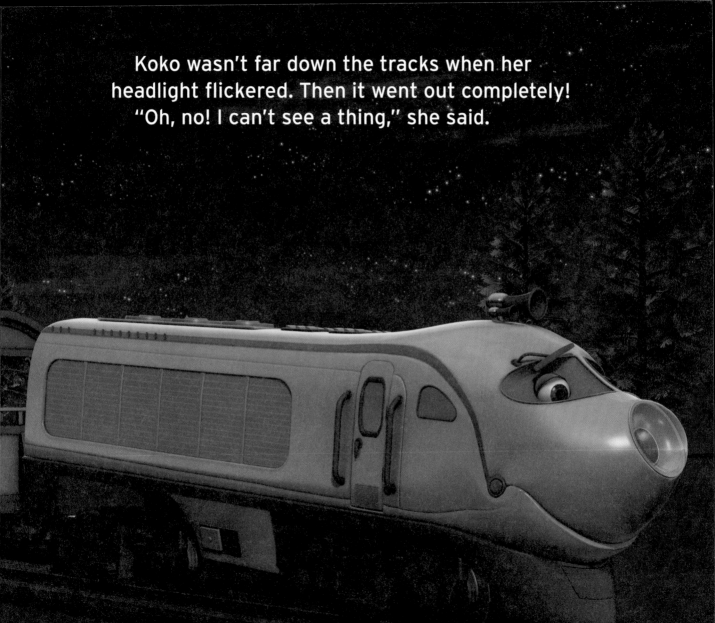

Koko wasn't far down the tracks when her headlight flickered. Then it went out completely! "Oh, no! I can't see a thing," she said.

Koko sat in the dark wondering what to do. Then she heard an owl hoot.

"Wait a minute," she said. "Nocturnal animals use their different senses to get around at night."

Koko crept forward along the dark tracks. She took a deep breath. "I can *smell* flowers," she said. "I remember now—turn at the flowers!"

Koko traveled down the dark tracks. Then she heard the sound of rippling water.

"I can *hear* the stream," she said. Her wheels rumbled under her. "And I can *feel* the bridge."

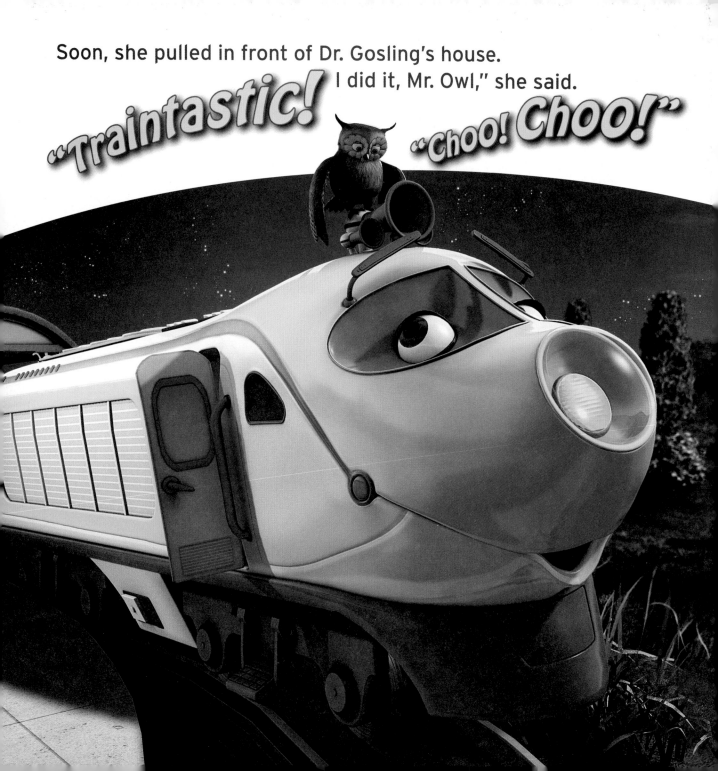

Koko brought Dr. Gosling back to the Safari Park as Wilson came rushing along.

"Koko, I have a message for you!" said Wilson. "Morgan said your bulb needs changing!"

Koko laughed. "Too late, Wilson!"
"Why don't you tell Wilson all about your nocturnal adventure while I take care of our very special delivery," said Dr. Gosling.

It was early in the morning when Dr. Gosling returned.
"It's a baby girl!" announced the doctor.

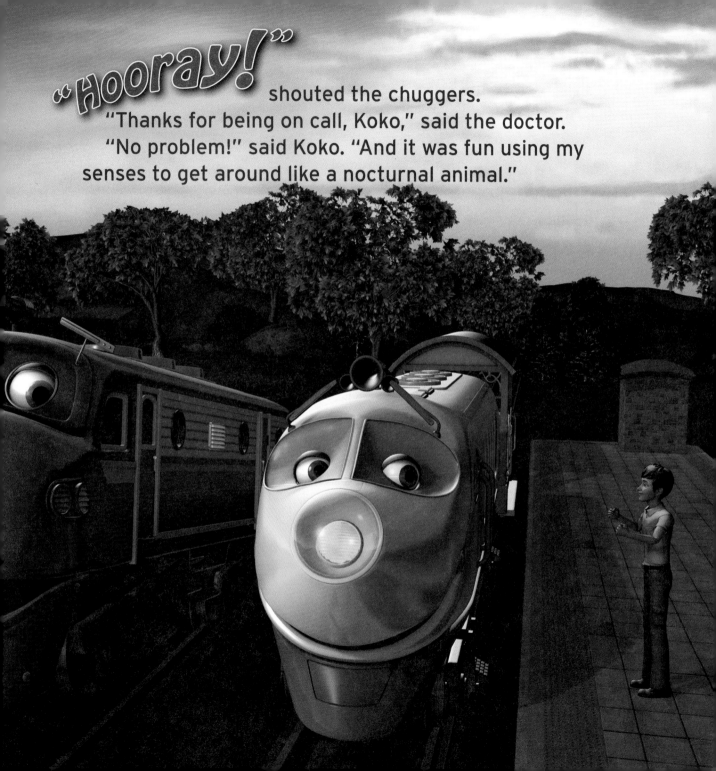

"Hooray!" shouted the chuggers.

"Thanks for being on call, Koko," said the doctor.

"No problem!" said Koko. "And it was fun using my senses to get around like a nocturnal animal."

"I think nocturnal animals are amazing," said Koko.

Just then, the owl flew in and landed on the tracks above.

"Whoo? Whoo?" asked the owl.

Koko looked up and smiled. "Who? Why, you! That's who!"

The chuggers and Dr. Gosling all laughed.